THE DOMINATRIX

AN EROTIC ADVENTURE

VICTORIA RUSH

VOLUME 12

JADE'S EROTIC ADVENTURES - BOOK 12

COPYRIGHT

You can be anyone you want online...

NAKED YOGA

AN EROTIC ADVENTURE

VICTORIA RUSH

Mula Bandha is for lovers...

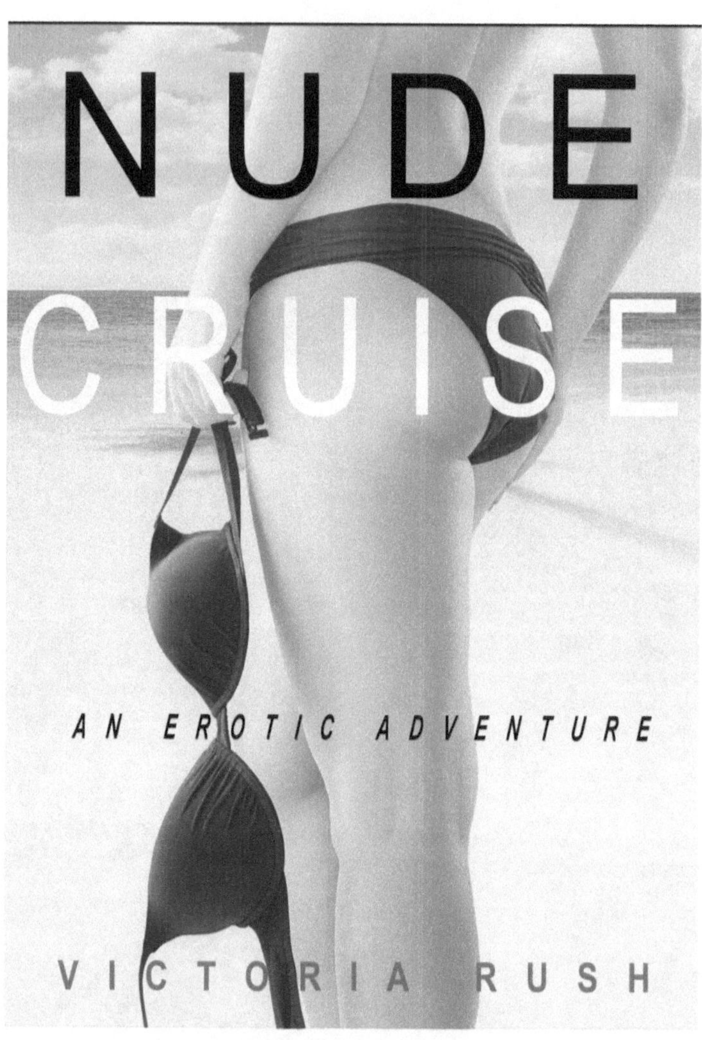

Some people get wet on a cruise for different reasons...

Books 6 - 10 in the bestselling series - now 60% off.

For the uninhibited...

1

BRAVE NEW WORLD

After my personal training sessions ended, I felt a new void in my sex life. Kate was incredibly hot and sexy and had pushed me past my limits in so many ways. She'd not only helped me restore my youthful body shape, she'd helped me realize that I could accomplish anything with the right motivation and workout plan.

But there was something else missing. I missed her guidance, her *commands*. There was something about the way she directed me through my paces that I found exhilarating and arousing. Even though she'd set me up with a self-directed routine to maintain my muscle tone, it wasn't nearly as much fun without her sexy body standing next to me, barking out orders to push out one more rep.

I needed a new life coach—one who'd push me beyond just my physical limits. I wanted a sex partner who'd fully take charge and *control* me. All I knew about BDSM was that it had something to do with bondage and domination. It was time to explore a new dimension to my sexuality.

I sat down in front of my computer and typed in the search box: *where to find a sexual master*. Near the top of the listings was a heading titled *Mistress Directory — Professional Mistresses and Dominatrix Contacts.* I clicked on the link and a website popped up with a gallery of sexy women dressed in provocative leather outfits holding whips and chains. I scrolled through the images until I saw a sexy redhead named Mistress Velvet.

When I opened her page, my eyes widened as the screen toggled between a series of full-screen photographs of the redhead in various stages of undress. Each pose revealed more and more of her voluptuous figure. In the first slide, she lay on a white leather settee in a red push-up bra and garters. Her large natural breasts overflowed her top, with the edge of her pink nipples peeking over the seam. In the next slide, she lay facedown in a shiny black body suit with her legs playfully elevated. I stared at her tight round ass, fantasizing about burying my face in her deep sensuous cleft. The third panel showed her on her hands and knees in a corset and nylons, with her knees suggestively splayed over an assortment of sex toys. My pussy fluttered imagining her lowering herself over me.

Even more tantalizing than her centerfold-perfect figure was her incredible beauty. Her dark eyes peered at me under long eyelashes as her plump crimson lips pursed in a beckoning pout, her waist-length auburn hair cascading over every sensuous curve and valley of her magnificent figure. Whatever this vixen was selling, I wanted a piece of it. I clicked on her Profile tab where an introductory paragraph described her services:

Welcome to Velvet's Place. My name is Mistress Velvet, the supreme Sex Goddess and Dominatrix. My mission is to deliver the ultimate sensual experience and take you to new heights of pleasure through my unique style of sexual domination. I'm highly experienced with most fetishes and forms of BDSM. My specially-equipped pleasure chamber is equipped with state-of-the-art bondage furniture and stimulation equipment designed to tease and arouse you until you beg for mercy. Call now or click the chat box below for more information...

Bondage furniture? Stimulation equipment?

I had no idea what she had in mind, but I liked the idea of teasing me until I begged for mercy. By the time I finished reading her profile, my panties were soaked all the way through imagining what it would be like to be her sex slave. I scanned toward the bottom of the page and clicked on the chat box, hoping somebody would be available at this late hour. My fingers hesitated over the keyboard, unsure how to initiate the discussion.

Is anyone there? I typed.

After a few seconds, three dots popped up in the reply window, indicating someone was responding on the other end.

Hello! someone named Velvet replied. *Welcome to Velvet's Place. How can we stimulate your senses today?*

Is this Mistress Velvet? I responded, hardly believing my luck getting hold of the proprietor on such short notice.

It is indeed. Although some people like to call me Goddess, Master, or Glaminatrix Velvet. I'm here to please. What's your kink?

What's my kink?! I thought, sitting back in surprise. *How do I respond to that kind of invitation?*

Well I'm kind of new to this whole thing, I typed, *so I'm not sure what to look for. I just kind of like the idea of someone 'taking charge' in the bedroom.*

Look no further, Velvet replied. *Though I don't do outcalls.*

And my sex chamber resembles more of a dungeon than a boudoir.

That sounds kind of scary. Is there any kind of torture or pain involved with your services?

Torture is in the eye of the beholder, she responded. *I inflict just enough pain to elevate your perception of pleasure. The withholding of pleasure can be exquisitely agonizing in its own right. By the time I finish with you, I guarantee you'll reach new heights of ecstasy.*

Just enough pain? Withholding of pleasure? It sounded like she was going to place me in some kind of torture rack. But she definitely had my interest. As I imagined her teasing and punishing me, I unzipped my jeans and thrust my fingers under my panties and began to play with my clit.

What kind of tools and restraints do you use? I typed. *Can I stop it if it gets too intense?*

Not to worry, Velvet replied. *When you arrive at my chamber, we will carefully discuss your interests and boundaries, then your session will be custom-designed to meet your individual needs. All your limits will be respected in a safe, mutually agreed upon way so your enjoyment is guaranteed. We'll sign a mutually binding waiver, and every session will be recorded to ensure everyone's rights are respected.*

Recorded? I suddenly had visions of my kinky S&M session going viral over the internet.

What do you do with the recording? I wouldn't want any of my intimate details being shared with the public...

It's for our mutual protection. I use old-school analog tape, so nothing can be copied. Upon satisfactory completion of the session, the tape is yours to keep. Many of my clients enjoy watching replays of our engagement to relive the moment long after they leave. No other record of the proceedings is taken beyond this.

I paused for a moment. Making a tape actually made a lot of sense. I could see how these sessions could get out of control from both sides, and having a record of the proceedings would ensure quick legal recourse if either party had a grievance. This Mistress Velvet was smart *and* sexy. My hand began moving faster between my legs at the thought of watching myself on videotape with the sexy redhead.

Will I be restrained? I enquired.

Half of the fun of BDSM is not being in control. I have special bondage chairs and harnesses that limit your range of mobility. I will stimulate you with a variety of appendages including whips and feathers and other sensual equipment. Sometimes it's more fun not being able to touch yourself or your partner while the final consumption is withheld.

Whips and feathers? The idea of being teased and tortured by someone while holding off the final release was getting me increasingly worked up. I spread my legs further apart, beginning to feel the pleasure radiating through my body.

Do you leave—marks? I typed with one hand.

Just minor localized inflammation in the form of temporary welts, she said. *I use a special leather whip that doesn't cut the skin. I think you'll find there's nothing like a little pain to heighten the feeling of pleasure.*

I stabbed at the keys while rubbing myself with increasing intensity.

So there'll be opportunities to experience pleasure as well?

Yes, Velvet replied. *It's just that it will be on my terms, and when I choose to allow it.*

Damn. I like the sound of that. I strummed my clit faster at the thought of her bringing me to the height of pleasure, only to make me beg for release.

So I'll be tied up?

Absolutely. I'll have you bound and stretched as wide as your body will allow so I can have my way with you.

Fuck me, I thought. I tore off my jeans and panties and thrust my fingers into my steaming tunnel. This Velvet goddess was already torturing me online.

Will I be able to touch you?

Only insofar as I take the initiative to touch you first. I enjoy touching my clients' bodies and having them touch me. But there will be limited ways in which you'll be able to engage with your hands and your feet while you're bound in the harness.

I smiled at the thought of Velvet having her way with me while I could only watch.

So you get off watching me squirm in restraints?

Absolutely. That's what being the domme is all about. As my slave, your role is to satisfy any of my curiosities and sexual whims. My clients get off just as much watching me get sexually aroused as when they finally have a chance to achieve release themselves.

The thought of watching this sexy redhead pleasure herself while I helplessly looked on elicited the familiar pangs of escalating pleasure from my core.

Do allow your clients to satisfy themselves in the end? I panted, stabbing spastically at the keyboard.

Yes, in a matter of speaking. But I'm the one who's always in control. Your release comes on my terms with my choice of apparatus. I assure you that after an hour of teasing and gentle torturing, your climax will be like no other.

"God! I" gasped, as my orgasm suddenly took hold of me. The image of this sexy redhead fucking me with some kind of contraption while I whimpered for release wrapped up in a ball of chains took me over the edge. I jerked softly in my chair as the waves of passion consumed me, reading what she'd written.

I believe you, I typed, pecking at the keys.

I paused for a moment to consider the next steps.

What are your rates and how soon are you available?

I charge four hundred dollars per hour, with a fifty percent deposit payable on booking and the remainder due at the start of the session. I'm booked solid for this week except for a small window this Saturday between ten a.m. and noon. If you'd like to reserve this spot, please fill in your online profile and complete the credit card details under the bookings tab.

That works for me, I typed. *If you can fit me into your Saturday slot, this is much appreciated.*

I'll block it off pending completion of your payment. May I ask your first name so I'll know who to expect?

I paused, contemplating whether to give her my real name.

It's Jade, I said, using the pseudonym that had become so intimately intertwined with my real identity.

Outstanding, Velvet replied. *Girls are a real treat from my usual parade of uptight guys.*

I smiled, knowing that she had a strong affinity for women.

See you Saturday, Velvet, I typed. *I mean Mistress Velvet,* signing off with a winking kiss emoji.

Saturday morning wasn't the only slot of hers I planned to fit into, I thought, as my juices dripped down over my hand still inserted deep inside my tunnel.

2

BONDAGE

On Saturday morning, I drove to Mistress Velvet's studio with a mix of trepidation and excitement. I was intrigued about being with a more dominant sexual partner, but I definitely felt uneasy about the idea of being tied up. As long as I remained in her clutches, I'd be completely at the mercy of someone who professed to enjoy inflicting pain.

As I drove across town, I kept shaking my head, unsure if I wanted to go through with it. I told myself that I'd check out her operation and that if I wasn't feeling entirely comfortable, I'd walk away. We'd have a long conversation about ground rules, and even if it ate into a portion of my paid session time, I needed to be sure I'd have final control over what happened to my body.

But something told me that this dominatrix was far more interested using me for her *own* pleasure than in watching someone else suffer. Anybody who was that concerned about protecting her safety with written contracts and session recordings must have long ago learned where to draw the line. The closer I got to her address, the tighter my thighs squeezed together, pinching my buzzing clit.

When my car's navigation system indicated that I'd arrived at my final designation, I looked around trying to locate Mistress Velvet's storefront. The street address comprised a long strip mall and there was no visible signage revealing her service location. I drove into the half-empty parking lot and stopped my car in front of the indicated unit number. A large plate-glass window covered the storefront with closed horizontal blinds.

Something didn't feel right. Everything was just too quiet and secluded. It would be the perfect location to torture and hold someone captive while you had your way with them. I was just about to turn around and drive away when I saw a young mother and child enter another shop a couple of doors down. I looked up and read the adjacent signs. There was a health clinic and a pet store on either side of the unmarked address. As a steady stream of patrons began to file in and out of the stores, my heart rate slowly returned to normal.

I got out of my car and walked up to the unmarked door to Unit Fourteen. Peering through the glass, I saw the familiar logo of Mistress Velvet dressed up in a naughty bodice riding a unicorn. Near the bottom of the sign was an arrow pointing down a long flight of stairs.

Of course she wouldn't broadcast her services for just any random passerby, I thought. *Who knows what kind of weirdos this kind of operation would attract? This is exactly the kind of service that should be by appointment only.*

I pulled on the handle and found it locked. I squinted at the side of the door and saw a small buzzer with a hand-written note reading *Press for Attendant.* I pressed the button and after a few seconds a female voice responded.

"Hello?" the voice said.

"My name is Jade," I replied. "I have a ten a.m. appointment with Mistress Velvet."

The door clicked and made a loud buzzing sound, and I pulled it open and scampered inside. The place had a strange musky scent, like a gym with slight undertones of lavender. The long flight of stairs led down to a closed door with a larger sign displaying Mistress Velvet's emblem. I walked down the steps and hesitated in front of the heavy door. There was a small peephole at eye height and I rapped on the surface with my knuckles.

A shadow flickered behind the peephole, then the door swung open. The beautiful redhead from Mistress Velvet's website smiled at me wearing a shiny vinyl trench coat with black fishnet stockings and high heels. Her huge breasts thrust against the reflective coating as her long curly locks cascaded over her shoulders. She was even more beautiful in the flesh, with high cheekbones, full pouty lips, and dark penetrating eyes.

"Welcome, Jade," she said, motioning me into the room. "I've been expecting you. Step into my dungeon."

When I entered the room, my eyes opened as wide as saucers. An assortment of whips and chains hung across the exposed brick walls. In each of the four corners rested a strange padded contraption. One could have passed for a conventional massage table, except for the wrist and leg cuffs strapped to either end. In the next corner stood a long padded board balancing on some kind of see-saw apparatus, with long leather straps running across the width of the board in one foot intervals. In the opposite corner rested a tall wooden throne-type chair with metal arm and foot restraints. In the final corner lay some kind of leather harness with a jumble of hopes and chains. Near the middle of the room, a long lever extended up from the floor, directly under a series of hooks and pulleys hanging down from the ceiling. If it weren't for a lone table holding an assortment of dildos and sex toys, I would have thought I was in some kind of medieval torture chamber.

"I see why you call this a *dungeon*," I said, nodding my head slowly. "It looks like more of a torture chamber."

"Everybody's a little taken back the first time they see my sex palace," the redhead nodded. "It looks scarier than it really is. I assure you, everything in this boudoir is designed to take you to new heights of pleasure."

"Only mine?" I said, noticing a huge strap-on dildo resting on the sex toy table.

"That depends on the client," she said, running her eyes up and down my body. "Under the right circumstances, we *both* can have a little fun."

I peered around the room at the assortment of bondage paraphernalia and narrowed my eyes.

"This is my first time doing something like this," I said. "Do you mind if we take a few minutes to discuss exactly what will be involved before we begin?"

"Of course," Velvet nodded. "I'd have it no other way. There are a few necessary preliminaries. Just keep in mind that I have another appointment at eleven. So we'll want to dispense with the formalities as quickly as possible in order to give you the maximum attention you deserve."

"Is there somewhere we can sit down?" I said. "I mean other than the torture rack or the throne chair?"

"Absolutely," Velvet chuckled, motioning in the direction of the sex toy table. "There are some comfortable chairs in this corner."

Velvet opened a collapsible chair and waited for me to sit down before sitting kitty-corner across the table. When she lifted her leg to cross her knees, I caught a fleeting glimpse of a black garter between her legs.

"What concerns do you have that I can assuage?"

"Well, mostly," I began tentatively, "I'm concerned about being tied up and having no ability to—*defend myself*. Will I be able to stop the proceedings at any time if I begin to feel uncomfortable?"

"Of course," she said, batting her long dark eyelashes. "We live in a civilized culture, after all. You'll always have the final say. I'm here to make you feel stimulated and excited, not to inflict unmitigated pain."

"So all I have to do is say 'stop' or 'no' when I want it to stop?"

"Technically, yes. Though I prefer each client to have a more elegant code word to terminate the proceedings. Just keep in mind that if you choose to deny me for any reason, that will automatically end the session and you won't be eligible for any refund of unused time. What would you like your code word to be?"

I paused to think of something less harsh than simply 'stop'.

"How about arrêtez? It means the same thing in French."

"That'll work," Velvet nodded. "But try to use it sparingly, since you can only say it once. I think you may find that the less control you have and the more uncomfortable you feel, the more invigorating the session will be. The whole point of BDSM is in giving complete control to your domme and in embracing the slave role."

My pussy pulsed at the mention of the word slave. I kept staring at the giant strap-on dildo on the other end of our table, thinking what Velvet had in mind for me.

"I understand," I nodded. "Where do we begin?"

Velvet reached into a drawer and passed a piece of paper and a pen across the table.

"I'll just need you to sign this waiver. And your credit card to process the rest of your payment."

"Of course," I said, reaching into my purse and passing her my card.

As Velvet processed my payment, I quickly scanned the contract. It was mostly standard boilerplate, limiting liability in the event of a dispute over the nature of services rendered. I was happy to see the clause referencing the recording of the proceedings and that I would be given the only tape upon successful completion of the session. The contract reiterated that Mistress Velvet would have complete and total authority to do whatever she pleased with me, so long as I didn't utter the agreed upon code word.

"Does everything appear satisfactory?" Velvet said, handing me the credit card voucher to sign.

"Yes, I think so," I said. "Although I'm a little confused by what 'satisfactory completion' of the session means."

"That's more for my protection than yours. It simply means that as long as I'm not physically threatened or harmed, you'll be given possession of the recording upon completion of the session. Not that I'm worried about you. But some of my male clients like to play pretty rough." Velvet pointed to a dark glass window on the far wall of the room. "Until then, everything will be securely filmed behind that wall."

I looked at the dark window and chuckled nervously.

"How do I know there isn't also some weirdo peeping at us behind that wall?"

"Fair question," Velvet said, beckoning me toward the door. "I like to be completely transparent at all times."

She punched in a code on the keypad lock, then swung

the door open for me to look inside. I peered into the closet-sized room and saw an old VHS video camera on a tripod, pointed toward the window.

"I like your style, Miss Velvet," I said, appreciating her abundance of caution.

"Shall we begin then?"

"Yes, I feel comfortable now."

Velvet stepped into the video room and pressed a button on the side of the camera and a red light begin to flash. Then she pulled the door closed and we returned to the sex toy table, where I signed the contract.

"Right then," she said, suddenly changing her tone. "From this point forward, you are to address me only as Mistress Velvet or Master. I will refer to you simply as Slave. Repeat the code word that you wish to use to cease all proceedings one last time. In the absence of this code word, you are to obey all of my commands. Is that understood?"

"Yes—Master," I smiled. "The code word is arrêtez."

"Good," Velvet said. "Now strip off all your clothes."

"Everything?"

"Everything."

I unbuttoned my blouse and slowly pulled it off my shoulders.

"Where shall I put them?" I said, looking at Velvet demurely.

"Hand them to me. I'll place them in a safe location."

I handed Velvet my blouse then unclasped my bra and passed it to her. Although she maintained a steely expression as she peered back and forth across my naked breasts, the quickening pace of her breathing as evidenced by her heaving breasts above her corset, betrayed her excitement.

"Now your pants," she ordered, glancing below my waist.

I unzipped my jeans and lowered them slowly to the

floor. Then I pulled off my sneakers and handed them to her. Finally, I pulled down my panties and held them out with an outstretched arm.

"What about you?" I said, running my eyes over her curvaceous figure hidden under her trench coat.

"I'm the one giving orders here, slave," she barked. "Now stand still while I appraise your figure."

She ran her eyes up and down my body, pausing for a long moment to stare at my bald hips and mound, then again at my nipples, which seemed to get harder and more erect the longer she stared at them.

"Not too shabby," she said, narrowing her eyes. "Now turn around."

I turned one-hundred-and-eighty degrees and stared at the dark window, smiling for the video camera.

"Spread your legs shoulder width apart and bend over ninety degrees."

As I followed Velvet's command, I felt the moisture beginning to accumulate on the inside of my labia.

"Very nice," she said. "Now turn around and face me again, with your legs spread shoulder width apart."

I turned around, and Velvet lowered her head to gaze at the bare folds of skin outlining my pussy.

"You'll do fine," she said. "I'm going to have a lovely time using and abusing your girlish figure. Wait here while I retrieve your harness."

Velvet hung up my clothes on a hook next to some whips and chains, then she disappeared behind me where I heard some rustling of clothes and equipment. When she returned to face me, she'd taken off her trench coat and was carrying a tangled assortment of leather, ropes, and chains. She kneeled down on the floor and spread out the equipment into a star shape, with the ropes angling out in four directions from a perforated leather harness.

When she stood back up, I ran my eyes wildly over her body. Her D-cup breasts spilled over the top of a black leather half-corset, with her large brown nipples pointing sensuously toward me above the seam. Her waist tapered to a narrow midsection, before flaring to wide, curvy hips, framed by a crotchless black leather garter supporting fishnet stockings with long thin black straps running up the front of her bare thighs. Her pussy, like mine, was entirely bare, revealing a large nub between her legs. I sagged at my knees, gasping at her gorgeous body.

"Lie down on the harness," Velvet commanded, directing her eyes to the floor.

"Can I just—" I pleaded, wanting a few more seconds to take in her magnificent figure.

"Lie down!" she commanded.

"Yes, Master," I demurred, kneeling down on the floor. "How do you want me—"

"Place your ass at the bottom of the harness, then lie back with your head toward the ropes. I'll take care of the rest."

I did as I was told, lying back against the cold perforated leather. The harness looked like a small hammock with large holes to permit maximum access to the recliner's skin. Velvet kneeled down and straddled my waist, and my pussy throbbed as I envisioned her rubbing herself against me. But instead she reached over my head and grabbed the ropes splayed out on the floor and began wrapping them tightly around my tits. She encircled each breast with the nylon cord, then ran a figure eight across the front of my chest and tied the two ends securely around the back of my neck.

My eyes widened at the thought of having a rope tied around my neck, but I began to relax when I realized the pressure point was behind my shoulders rather than over my throat. I peered down at my tightly bound boobs, noticing how they'd already swelled from the constricted circulation. My areolas had turned a dark shade of purple and my nipples stood out almost a full inch, tingling in arousal.

Velvet paused for a moment to appraise her handiwork then peered into my eyes with a sexy grin.

"Do you like that, my sexy little slave?" she purred. She grabbed my tits with her two hands and squeezed them roughly. "Because your nipples are definitely saying yes."

"Yes," I squeaked, arching my hips to press against her body.

Velvet spread her knees wider apart, placing her full weight on my abdomen, thumping my body back onto the floor. Then she lowered her head and sucked hard on each of my erect nipples for a few seconds, making a loud popping sound each time she removed her mouth. Her wet pussy writhed against my bare stomach as she pinned her body over mine.

"Fuck yes!" I exclaimed, letting her know in no uncertain terms that I was enjoying her attention.

Then she shimmied her hips over my hard mound and hipbones, spreading her juices over my midsection like she was marking me.

"I'm going to have a lot of fun with you before we're finished," she said. "But first I need to get you properly restrained so I can have my way with you."

She waddled up my body until her pussy rested just above my face, then she grabbed my arms and tied the ropes at the top of the harness tightly around my wrists. Then she threaded the loose ends through two eyelets and tied secure knots to hold my arms high above my head. When she finished binding my hands to the harness, she peered down to see me staring at her glistening labia. I extended my tongue trying to touch her throbbing clit, but she kneeled just far enough away for me not to reach her.

"You want to lick my pussy, slave?" she taunted. "You'll have to beg for it. But don't worry, there will be plenty of opportunities for you to satisfy me soon enough. Let's get those pretty little legs of yours pulled up with your arms. I want to have unfettered access to your sweet, moist kitty."

Velvet lifted her knee and turned around so she was straddling me in the other direction. She leaned forward, revealing her pink rosebud and dripping labia. When I lifted my head trying to reach her, she shifted her body in the other direction, toward my hips. She paused for a moment over my bound breasts and rubbed her pussy over each of my distended nipples until both of my tits were thoroughly coated with her sex juices. There was something incredibly sexy about her spreading her wetness all over my prostrated body while I could only stand there and watch. My hips twisted and convulsed, trying vainly to produce some friction against my aching clit.

When she reached my midsection, she straddled my hips again and titled forward at the waist, giving me another premium view of her tight rosebud and wide-open lips. Then she grabbed my legs and wound the other two ends of the loose ropes around my ankles while spreading my legs apart. When she finished, she stood up and pulled the ropes as far as she could toward my head, binding my ankles to my hands. I was now stretched as far into an accordion position as my body allowed, with my legs splayed and pulled behind my head. I looked between my legs and saw that my pussy was wide open, with my labia spread apart and my juices dripping down the crack of my ass.

"Now we're talking," Velvet smiled, standing over me, nodding approvingly. "It looks like you're already getting excited about the idea of being hog-tied for my amusement. But you haven't seen anything yet."

She stood over me for a moment, straddling my waist in her six-inch stilettos, then stepped slowly up toward my head. I peered nervously out of the corner of my eyes, fearing she might pinch my skin with her sharp heels, but she simply sneered as she got closer and closer to my breasts. When she reached my armpits, she spread her legs on either side of my shoulders and paused to let me peer up her long and magnificent body. Her legs seemed to go on forever, and above the sensuous cleft between her legs, her tits jutted out like ripe melons from the dark stem of her corset.

Her pussy was glistening in obvious excitement, and as I watched her juices begin to run down the inside of her thighs, I hoped they might eventually reach the sides of my body. But just as I envisioned she might let me have a small taste of her body, she stepped over my head and grabbed the top of my harness and fastened three chains with hooks to the top and two sides of my harness. Then she lifted the three ends of the chains toward a large metal hook hanging from the ceiling.

"What the—?" I muttered, realizing she intended to lift me up onto the hook.

"That's right," Velvet sneered. "I'm going to hang you from the rafters like a piece of meat. Then you'll really see who's in charge here."

She connected the ends of each chain to the large over-head hook, then she grabbed the lever poking up from the floor and began thrusting it forward and back. The slack in the chains tightened, and I began to feel myself lifting off the floor. Most of my weight was supported by the black leather harness, but I could definitely feel my arms and legs stretched tighter and wider with each pull of the lever. When my ass elevated to Velvet's hip level, she stopped cranking the lever and looked down at me. Every part of my body was pulled as high and far apart as possible. I peered down my midsection, seeing my tits squeezed into tight pyramids and my hips curled up toward my face, revealing the separated parts of my puffy lips spread into a wide and gleaming crevasse.

Velvet reached up onto the two chains supporting the sides of my harness and suddenly pulled them down, angling my body forty-five degrees forward.

"Do you like that, my sweet?" she said, looking deep into my eyes, stepping forward and rubbing her bare mound tantalizingly against my splayed pussy.

"Yes, Master," I said. "Please fuck me now. I want you to have your way with me."

"Oh I will, my slave. Don't you worry. When I'm finished with you, I'll have sprayed myself all over your tight little body and you'll have licked every square inch of me."

Velvet walked slowly around my suspended body until she was standing behind my head. Then she reached up and yanked down on the chain supporting the other end of my harness. I suddenly tilted forty-five degrees in the other direction, until my head dangled just under her dripping pussy. Then she turned around and planted her ass on my face.

"Lick my rosebud, slave," she commanded. "I want you to clean me with your tongue."

3
____

DOMINATION

For a moment, I panicked. I imagined Mistress Velvet subjecting me to an increasingly demeaning series of sex acts where I'd have no ability to extract myself from my helpless state. My face was buried in the cleft of her ass and I had very little freedom of movement. I considered twisting my head and crying out my safe word, but then I remembered the contract said my session would end as soon as I did. I'd signed up for this crazy idea; the least I could do was give her a chance to explore my limits.

Besides, her anus didn't smell nearly as bad as I thought. In fact, it smelled kind of pleasant, with hints of lemongrass and vanilla. Velvet had obviously already cleaned herself with some kind of scented soap.

Of course, I thought, *she wouldn't make someone lick her unclean ass. That would be a little over the top. This was a business after all, and her success relied in large part upon repeat business.*

"What's the matter, slave?" Velvet said, rubbing her cheeks against my face. "Have you never licked a beautiful woman's rosebud before? You never know if you might like it until you try. Don't worry—I won't bite. It's time to pay tribute to your master and kiss my ass."

I tentatively extended my tongue and felt the fleshy folds on the insides of her cheeks. It was soft and smooth, not rough and gritty like I imagined. There was no appreciable taste other than the slightly salty flavor of fresh sweat that I'd experienced while running on the treadmill at the gym. Beyond the faint smell of lemony soap, the only scent that penetrated my nostrils was a sexy musk aroma, similar to the pleasant smell of a woman's freshly washed pussy.

"That's right, sweetheart," Velvet purred. "Lick my ass. Run your tongue over my rosebud and make your master feel good."

I titled my head up a few degrees, moving my tongue closer to her anus. The closer I got to her puckered hole, the more I could feel the gentle folds of her skin on my sensitive tongue. When I reached the deepest part of her pit, I closed my eyes and pursed my lips to prevent the intrusion of any undesired elements. But to my surprise, there was no change in taste or smell, and I found myself enjoying the sensation of probing her most intimate parts with my tongue. Before long, I was swirling and lapping up her bare flesh like an ice cream cone.

"Now you've got the idea," Velvet panted, as she pressed her ass down further and began to hump my face. "Be a good little slave and lick my ass all the way from my tailbone to my pussy."

As Velvet tilted her hips up and down, giving me freer access to the full length of her undersides, I opened my mouth and savored the sexy mixture of my saliva and her bodily fluids coating her ass. Every few seconds, she'd angle her hips far enough forward to allow me to see her rubbing her clit furiously with her right hand. Seeing her touch herself while I licked her most sensitive areas sent a charge through me, and I buried my face deeper into her chasm as I motorboated her tight ass cheeks.

"Yeah baby," Velvet moaned. "That's what I'm talking about. Have your way with my ass. Make Mistress Velvet cum all over your face."

My eyes suddenly flung open in surprise.

She was going to let me make her cum this way?

This bondage thing had already exceeded my expectations. The feeling of pleasuring my partner while balled up in restraints suspended from the ceiling was more erotic than I ever imagined. When Velvet shifted her ass down my face and positioned her soaking pussy over my mouth, I moaned into her crevasse.

"Do you like that, slave?" she said. "Do you like burying your face in my sweet pussy? Lick my cunt and taste my juices. Hold still while I fuck your tongue with my slit."

I extended my tongue as far as I could into her hole, curling it to make it firmer and harder. She began to flex her knees up and down, and I penetrated her deeper. Her labia spread wider and wider apart until my entire mouth and chin was embedded in her cavern.

"Fuck, yes," Velvet moaned. "Fuck my pussy with your tongue. Make Mistress Velvet gush all over your pretty face."

As the pace of Velvet's movement on my face increased with the volume of her commands, I knew it wouldn't be long before she came. I pressed my tongue deeper inside her, trying to reach her G-spot. Suddenly, she tilted her hips down and I felt a fleshy proboscis snap into my mouth. For a moment, I was unsure what she had inserted into me until I felt the telltale throbbing of firm flesh.

It was her clitoris. She had a huge, oversized clit. It must have been almost three inches long, and freestanding like a man's cock. Firm and pointy, it felt like a red chili pepper in my mouth. I'd never seen or felt a woman's clit like this, and as I sucked it deeper into my mouth, my own clit pulsed in excitement.

"Yeah, baby," Velvet moaned. "Suck Momma's big cock. Do you like my big fat clit?"

"Umm-hmm," I murmured, wrapping my tongue around the shaft and head-banging her with my face.

"Suck it, slave," Velvet panted. "Suck my flute until I come. I'm getting close."

I could feel her juices streaming all over my face as she face-fucked me with her meaty phallus. I opened my eyes and saw her butt cheeks shaking in a spasm above me and knew that she was close. I began flicking my tongue over the sensitive end of her big clit, then she pulled out of me and planted her ass over my mouth.

"Fuck, yes!" she screamed. "Tease my anus while I come. Make your master cum, slave!"

As I flicked my tongue over her puckered opening, I watched with amazement as her hips writhed and shook over top of me. Her anus seemed to open slightly, and for a moment I worried that she intended to defecate on me in a final perverted denouement to our session. But instead, she pressed down harder onto my face and in one final thrust, let out a primal scream.

"Uhnnn," she groaned. "Fuck my anus, baby. Fuck my hole while I cum all over you."

I curled my tongue again and Velvet pressed it into her hole as her hips and buttocks shook in spastic delirium. To my surprise, I still didn't taste or smell any sign of unpleasantness, as I realized that she'd cleansed her insides also. I peered down between her cheeks and saw her long pointy clit flicking up and down in spastic jerks, like a man does when he comes. The multiple assault on my senses was simply too much, and I suddenly gushed a geyser out of my upturned pussy as I came hard watching and feeling her come.

"Oh! Oh! Oh!" Velvet moaned, as I felt her anus clamping down over my tongue in repeated contractions. This was something I'd never shared with anyone before, and I spasmed along with her for many long seconds before I felt my juices running back down along my elevated thighs and upturned ass. Velvet jerked and moaned with my face still buried in her ass, and I dribbled like a baby as my saliva and her pussy juices washed all over my face.

My first experience with bondage and domination felt more like a baptism than a persecution.

$$4$$

DENIAL

When Velvet finally finished cumming, she turned around and grabbed the sides of my head with two hands and pulled my face roughly into her snatch. I peered up at her still-erect clit with wide eyes, amazed at the size of her twitching womanhood.

"Good job, slave," she said. "You're a natural at this. You know how to give good head. Do you like my big girl-cock?"

"Yes," I murmured under the slick folds of her throbbing pussy.

"Do you want me to *fuck* you with it later?"

As I nodded my head enthusiastically, my pussy pushed out one last spasm of love nectar. Velvet peered up and noticed the coating of juices over my legs, then she narrowed her gaze and shook her head disapprovingly.

"What's that?" she said. "You didn't come too, did you? Because I haven't given my permission. You're only supposed to satisfy *me*."

"I'm sorry," I said. "I couldn't help it. It was just too much of a turn-on watching you—"

"*I'm* the one who decides when you're allowed to feel any pleasure. You've been a naughty girl, and now you'll have to pay the price for breaking the rules."

Velvet paced to the far wall where she removed some items hanging on the hooks on the exposed brick surface, then she lifted a collapsed director's chair and placed it on the floor in front of me. She unfolded the chair and placed the paraphernalia on the seat, then reached down and lifted two stainless steel clasps and held them up in front of my face.

"You'll have to experience a little bit of pain to pay amends for stealing some unauthorized pleasure. Do you know what these are?"

"Um," I hesitated, looking at the devices with wide eyes. "I can guess—"

"That's right," she said. "They're nipple clamps. This will teach you what it feels like to disobey your master."

Velvet pressed the front of my harness down a few inches as my head tilted toward the floor. Then she squeezed the clasps open one at a time and placed them over my erect nipples and slowly spread her fingers. As the pressure of the clamps squeezed tighter and tighter against my nipples, I groaned in pain.

"Does that hurt, baby?" Velvet said in a taunting voice. "Don't worry, you'll get used to it soon enough. You might even grow to like it. Many of my clients find the pain only heightens the pleasurable feeling of being bound and controlled."

I grimaced as I watched my nipples turn a ruddy shade of purple from the constricted circulation. But inside, I had to admit seeing the metal clamps standing firmly attached to my erect nipples was turning me on even more.

"But don't get too excited about having your erogenous

parts stimulated," she said. "Because I have so many other ways to punish you."

Velvet grabbed the side of my harness and swung me around one-hundred-and-eighty degrees until my ass was facing her once again. Then she pulled the front of the harness down so I was tilted up just enough for me to see her midsection. As I watched her still-throbbing woman-cock, for a moment I thought she intended to fuck me with it to teach me a lesson. But instead, she sat down on the director's chair and picked up a long wand that looked like some kind of horse whip. Staring between my legs, she snapped it in the air in front of my exposed pussy.

"That's a very pretty kitty you have," she said. "What kind of implements do you think it might accommodate for me today? I have such a broad selection of equipment..."

Velvet slapped the leather strands at the end of the wand on top of my chest, and I flinched as I watched the strands splay out across my breasts.

"Did that hurt, baby?" she said, pinching her eyebrows together in mock empathy. "Because we're just getting started."

She slowly pulled the whip down the front of my body until the leather strands ran between my legs and spilled over my pussy. I shuddered at the first sensation of direct contact against my private parts and raised my hips begging for more.

"Do you like that?" Velvet said, raising an eyebrow.

She raised the whip over her head and held it menacingly over my quivering snatch. Then she suddenly arced the wand to the side of my hips and snapped the leather straps against the bottom of the harness. I yelped when I felt the sting of the straps on my bare ass through the holes in the harness and instinctively tilted my hips in the other direction.

"Sorry," Velvet teased. "I didn't mean to strike you quite so—*softly*."

She snapped the whip again and struck me a few inches lower on my buttocks on the same side of the harness. I winced in pain and twisted the harness as far as I could away from her.

"There's nowhere you can go, my sweet," she said with a sneer. "You're just going to have to lie there and take your punishment. But don't worry, my whips are specially designed to inflict maximum pain with minimum bodily harm. This is an equestrian whip, designed with wide, smooth-edged strands of leather that won't puncture your skin. Doesn't it feel sublime?"

Velvet shifted the wand to her other hand and suddenly snapped the whip against the other side of my body. My body jerked from the unexpected attack on my unblemished side.

"I can't hear you," Velvet said, snapping the whip in the same area, stinging my left buttock cheek.

"Yes, Mistress," I groaned weekly.

Velvet snapped the whip harder, striking me on the same tender part that was still smarting from her last lash.

"Yes, Master," I squealed, louder.

I struggled to form the right words to describe the sensation.

"It feels...tender, yet sensitive. I see what you mean by heightening my sensations."

A wide smile formed on Velvet's lips.

"Exactly. Doesn't the pain so close to your most sensitive zones make you tingle all the more in other areas?"

"Yes Master," I said, unsure if by agreeing it would be more likely to increase or decrease her flogging.

"Well then, let's finish getting you properly tenderized. It will make the next stage all the more enjoyable."

"For you or for me?" I said, wondering what she had in store next.

"Silence!" Velvet barked. "I'll tell you when you can speak. Speak now!"

She snapped the whip three times in rapid succession against the underside of my harness, each time getting closer and closer to my exposed pussy. Each time I squealed out loud, half in real pain and half in overreaction, hoping she'd have mercy and strike me more softly.

For another minute or so, she struck me repeatedly, flogging the entire underside of my back and buttocks, until she leaned over and placed the whip on the floor. I was glad that she'd spared my front side, not least because my breasts were already tender from the clamps still pinching my tender and extended nipples.

Velvet glanced up at the clock on the adjacent wall, then reached down beside her chair to pick up a new object that was outside my line of sight. It was ten-forty. I couldn't imagine another twenty minutes of this kind of punishment before our session ended.

"Have you learned your lesson, slave?" she said. "Do you think you've felt enough pain for today?"

"Yes, Mistress," I said, wondering what she intended to do with our remaining time.

"Alright then," she said, suddenly standing up. She lifted her arm and waved a long feather boa in the air. "Let's see if we can torment you with a different kind of pain. Sometimes it's the softest of touches that can be the most cruel."

Velvet lowered the boa toward the floor and traced it along the sides of the harness as she walked slowly around my suspended body. I shivered at the soft sensation of the feather against the tender welts where she'd flogged me with the whip. When she reached the other side of my body, she placed the feather at the top of my head and slowly lowered it over my face. I closed my eyes, feeling the soft fringes flow over my cheeks and jaw, raising my chest instinctively to welcome it on the lower portion of my body. When she reached my neck, she angled the boa sideways and drew it across my throat in both directions. The feathers tickled me slightly, and I giggled softly.

"It tickles, does it?" Velvet said, smiling at me gently. "Maybe this will tickle your fancy even more."

She dragged the large boa slowly over my chest, stopping to encircle each of my clamped nipples with the most delicate touch. I arched my back, enjoying the exquisite softness juxtaposed against my stinging nipples enclosed in the tight clamps.

"There now," Velvet purred. "Doesn't that feel better? Mistress Velvet isn't all about pain, you know. Don't you agree that pleasant feelings are magnified in the presence of pain?"

"Yes," I sighed, rolling my breasts across the feather to increase the stimulation.

"Shall we test this theory by stimulating your more erogenous areas now?" she said, glancing in the direction of my upturned pussy.

"Yes please," I panted, tilting my aching pussy further up in the air.

Velvet chuckled as she moved the boa onto the undersides of my upturned legs. Then she slowly waved it down my thighs toward my throbbing snatch. Even though my back and buttocks were still smarting from the flogging she'd just meted out, the feeling of the soft feather on my untouched skin made the little hairs on my legs stand up in excitement. It was true what she'd said about pleasurable sensations being magnified in the presence of pain.

But when the boa reached the base of my thighs, instead of drawing it inward toward my pussy, she tilted her arm and drew it softly across my back. The feeling of the soft feather touching my painful welts somehow multiplied the tenderness of my skin, and I grimaced as she fluttered it over the inflamed surface.

"It's strange feeling pleasure and pain at the same time, isn't it?" Velvet said, smiling at my discomfort.

I nodded softly, not wanting to encourage her too much.

"Let's see if it feels any better on the untouched parts of your body," she said.

She dragged the feather along the underside of my body toward my buttocks, then drew it up between the crack of my ass and over my pussy. She watched my legs quivering as my pussy dribbled down my crease.

"Yes," Velvet smiled, noticing the wetness between my legs. "Your body seems to agree. Are those cries of sadness or pleasure?"

"Pleasure," I whimpered, as she tilted her hand up and down, drawing the feather up and down my folds. I wriggled my hips wildly, trying to increase the friction of the feather against my burning clit, but Velvet seemed to enjoy steering it just at the edge of my love button.

"Please," I blurted out, forgetting that I wasn't supposed to speak unless spoken to.

"Do you want *more*?" Velvet said, smiling at me with a sinister sneer. "Or would you like something a little *firmer* touching your pretty little twat?"

"Yes please," I nodded enthusiastically.

"Let's see if we can find something a little more —*satisfying*."

She leaned over and picked a new object off the seat of the director's chair. When she held it up for me to see, my eyes widened and my pussy pulsed uncontrollably. It was a Magic Wand, one of my favorite vibrating sex toys.

"You've used one of these before, I see," she said, plugging the device into an extension cord snaking from the wall.

I nodded softly, twisting my hips in a beckoning motion.

"Perhaps not quite the way I intend to use it though," she said.

Velvet flicked the ON switch on the side of the handle and the ball-shaped head of the vibrator began to buzz and shake. Then she leaned over and held the vibrating head against each of my nipple clamps. I gasped at the sensation of the snaps buzzing against my tender nubs.

"Pleasure and pain," Velvet smiled, looking into my eyes. "Isn't it exquisite?"

I nodded excitedly, rolling my body in excited convolutions.

"Something tells me you might like it even more somewhere *else*," she said, glancing at my twitching pussy.

She pressed the head of the wand against the underside of my knee and slowly traced it down my right thigh until it hovered next to my quivering labia. As I felt the vibrations radiating into my core, I twisted my hips to press the vibrator closer to my aching clit.

"Do you want more *direct* contact?" Velvet teased, peering into my eyes.

"Yes, Master," I moaned. "Please—Mistress."

"Your wish is my command."

She slowly lowered the vibrator until it sat between the

crack of my ass, then she pulled it forward until it rested over my anus. Feeling the vibrations directly against my rosebud while my pussy quivered in excitement was something I'd never experienced before. I began to feel the familiar urge rising up inside me and could have easily come from the stimulation to this sensitive area of my perineum, but Velvet suddenly lifted the wand off my skin when she noticed my breathing escalate.

"You see?" she said. "The anus is indeed an erogenous zone. It's not just *guys* who like to have that area stimulated. But it's too early to let you release all that pent-up energy. I have other plans for you."

I turned my head to glance at the clock on the wall. It read ten-fifty-five. There was only five minutes left in my scheduled session, and I was aching to come.

"Please, Mistress," I begged. "Let me come. I'm burning up inside."

Velvet sat down on the director's chair and lifted her thighs over the armrests, spreading her bare pussy apart.

"Is *this* what you want?" she said.

She placed the head of the magic wand over her slit then rubbed it up and down her opening, pausing for a long moment to stimulate her anus, then she pulled it back up and inserted the thick ball inside her dripping pussy. As she wiggled her hips and moaned softly, I watched her clit once again rise and extend from her body. When it had reached its full three-inch hard angry state, she pulled the vibrator out of her pussy and pressed it firmly against her twitching digit with two hands.

"Do you think you can come again, watching me get off?" she asked, peering at me through dewy eyes. "Because I'd like to watch you gush all over your thighs and ass while I come."

I shook my head, unsure if I could come again without direct stimulation. But the sight of Velvet jilling herself with two hands on the vibrating wand held against her big chili pepper clit, soon changed my mind. Within seconds, I felt the familiar pangs of a rising orgasm welling up within me, and I tilted my head to look at my twitching pussy lips.

"Yes, Master," I groaned. "I'll happily come with you."

"Good," she said. "This time I'm going to watch your rosebud pucker and spasm when you come. I'm getting close. Are you ready?"

"Yes," I panted, feeling the first waves of my orgasm beginning to wash over me. "I'm going to cum, Master."

"Uhnnn," Velvet moaned. "Cum with me, baby. Let me see your sweet hole smile and pucker for me. Here it comes!"

Velvet suddenly screamed out my name as her arm muscles tightened and she began jerking wildly in her chair.

"Jade!" she yelled. "Spray your cum all over your master's tits and cock. I'm cumming!"

As soon as Velvet uttered those words, I lost all control and my pussy and anus began clamping down hard, as all the built-up fluid inside my upturned pussy sprayed out in a wide arc directly in front of Velvet. As she spasmed in her chair, my juices spread all over her giant tits and girl-cock. For almost a full minute, the two of us faced each other, thrashing and moaning while we watched each other have one of the most powerful orgasms of our lives.

5

CONSUMMATION

After Velvet finally stopped cumming in her chair, she stood up and walked over to me. She placed her palms on the underside of my upturned legs then drew her hands down over my dripping skin and smeared my juices all over her breasts. As if winking at me, her big pink clit still stood on end, twitching between her legs.

"You're been a good girl," she said. "You know how to satisfy Mistress Velvet like a proper slave."

She noticed me glancing at her huge clit and smiled.

"But something tells me you're still not satisfied. Do you want something inside that pretty pussy to feel like a complete woman?"

"Yes," I said, peering up at the wall clock. It was two minutes before eleven. The last thing I needed was another client walking in and seeing me hanging in the air covered with my own sex juices.

"But aren't you expecting—"

"There's been a cancellation. I've got another free hour if

you'd like to use it. I'm willing to offer it for half the regular rate if you're interested."

Whether she'd told me earlier that she had another appointment to encourage me to take the last open slot of the week, didn't matter to me. Right now, I desperately needed to be fucked, and I would have paid twice the going rate if she'd demanded it.

"I'm definitely interested," I panted, swiveling my hips in front of her fluttering clit.

"Good," she said. "We can take care of the payment at the end of the session. Was there anything in particular you had in mind?"

I licked my lips as I stared at her giant twitching pudendum.

"I want you to fuck me with your big girl-cock," I said, spilling out my fantasy.

"I bet you do," Velvet said. "You've never been fucked by a real ladycock, have you?"

At this point, I was hardly in a position to quibble about whether any of my previous transgender experiences qualified.

"No," I said. "Please fuck me, Mistress Velvet. I want to feel you inside me while I cum all over your pretty clit."

Velvet hesitated for a moment while she ran her eyes over my bound-up body.

"We might be able to arrange that," she said. "But first, I want you to suck me. Let's see what kind of head my pretty slave can muster up for her master."

She swung the harness around again until my face was between her legs. Her vulva was slick with a mixture of our juices, and her large erect clit waved in the air above my mouth.

"First, I want to fuck your throat to remind you who's the master. If you're a good slave and make me cum hard enough, we'll see about filling that pretty little pussy of yours with an appropriate tool."

I was disappointed that she wasn't going to fuck me yet with her big clit, but I was excited about the prospect of feeling it inside my mouth. She stepped forward until she was standing directly over my face, then she tilted my head downwards and forced my jaw open. Then she thrust her wet chili pepper all the way into my cavity.

At first, I almost choked on the sudden intrusion, but when I realized that her cock wasn't long enough to touch the back of my throat, I relaxed and closed my lips around the shaft. It was strange feeling the pointy phallus in my mouth. It was thinner and shorter than other cocks I'd had, and it was comforting to know that she couldn't gag me with it or fill my mouth with salty cum. I wrapped my tongue around the fleshy stem and bobbed my head against her undercarriage, trying my best to give her a memorable blowjob.

"That's my girl," Velvet said. "Suck your master's girl-cock. Feel me twitching inside your pretty mouth."

She grabbed the sides of my head and pulled me harder against her vulva and began thrusting her cock deeper inside my mouth. Far from feeling used, there was something incredibly sexy about feeling another woman's wet vulva mashing against my face while she fucked my mouth like a man. As Velvet thrust her cock deeper inside me, I pursed my lips to increase the pressure on her shaft and began to swirl my lips around the pointed end.

"Fuck yes," Velvet panted. "Suck the head of my dick, slave. Just like that. Make your master cum in your mouth."

She tilted her hips down a few degrees to press deeper inside me, and I opened my eyes to see her buttocks spreading apart, revealing her twitching rosebud. As she increased the speed of her thrusting into my mouth, I could see her hole widening as she approached climax. I found it fascinating to watch this previously unexplored organ go through the same cycle of arousal, plateau, and orgasm that I was so familiar with from my own pussy.

Velvet's commands suddenly elevated in pitch and urgency, and I knew she was on the edge.

"Yes, Jade," she moaned. "I'm going to cum inside your pretty mouth.

"Ohhhh!" she suddenly groaned.

Although she wasn't cumming inside me like a regular man, there was no doubt that she was in the throes of a real orgasm, as I watched her pretty pucker spasm and clench in repeated strong contractions.

"Uh-Uh-Uh," she panted in synchronicity with each of her contractions.

I sucked as hard as I could on her twitching cock while she gushed all over my face and neck. The feeling of being prostrated underneath her while she had her way with me just added to the eroticism of the experience. Though I didn't come with her this time, my pussy throbbed and pulsed in sympathy with each of her contractions. I could feel myself leaking once again out my slit, and in my reclined state, my juices began running down my stomach and over my tightly bound breasts.

Velvet kept hold of my head, jerking softly against my face, until her rosebud finally stopped spasming, then she pulled out of me and held her twitching clit over my eyes. I watched in fascination as the pointy appendage jerked and throbbed with each new beat of her heart. She held herself over me for a moment, running her eyes all over my upturned body, nodding in approval.

"That was heavenly," she panted, still out of breath. "You sure know how to give good head, little girl. I think it's time you had a proper reward."

She peered up my body at my twitching hole.

"Are you ready to see what it feels like to have a big girl-cock inside your pussy now?"

"Yes, master," I said. "I'm so ready for you to fuck me."

"So am I," Velvet said. "I want to bury my dick deep in your cunny. Are you ready for me to fuck you like a man now?"

"Yes, master. Fuck me with your man-cock."

Velvet swung the harness around again, then angled it down until my hips were just under hers. I tilted my head up and was glad to have a clear line of sight all the way down her upper thighs. But instead of stepping forward and inserting her ladycock into my hole, she turned around and leaned over to wiggle her ass in my face.

What is it with this anal obsession of hers? I thought. As sexy as it was, I need some direct stimulation. *If she doesn't trib me or fuck me right now, I'll go out of my mind.*

As if reading my mind, Velvet suddenly lowered her hips onto mine and began swiping her wet lips over mine.

"God, yes," I moaned. "Rub your pussy against me, Miss Velvet. That feels so good."

"Mmm, yes," Velvet purred. "You're so wet. Your lips are so soft and puffy. Have you been getting pumped up watching Mistress Velvet having her way with you?"

"Yes," I panted. "I've been throbbing the whole time I've watched you. I'm ready to burst at the seams."

"I like the sound of that. Will you gush inside your

master's pussy this time? I want to feel you spray all over my ass when you cum."

"Fuck yes," I moaned. "I'm gonna squirt all over your pretty rosebud."

Velvet tilted her hips toward me, and I felt her clit slip inside me.

"Yes, master," I squealed, thrilled to finally feel her inside me. "Fuck me with your big ladycock."

As Velvet began humping my hips up and down, I tilted my head forward to watch her pointy appendage pistoning inside me. The feeling of having her hot clit inside me while she mashed her pussy lips against mine felt sublime. I'd been holding off for so long feeling any direct stimulation on my pussy that it didn't take long for the passion to quickly well up inside me.

"Mistress Velvet," I moaned. "You're going to make me cum soon. I can't hold it any longer. Fuck me hard with your big cock."

Velvet picked up the pace of her pounding against my vulva, then she tilted her hips down a bit further and I felt the tip of her pointy cock tickling my G-spot. My orgasm suddenly crashed over me with the power of a tsunami.

"Fuck, yes!" I screamed. "I'm cumming! Pound me, Mistress Velvet. Pound my sweet pussy while I cum all over your pretty cock and ass."

I tensed my neck muscles to keep my head tilted forward and watched a geyser erupt from my upturned pussy as I sprayed all over Velvet's tight pucker.

"Oh God," she screamed. "I feel you cumming all over my ass."

As she pressed her hips against me with one final thrust, her buttock muscles twitched and spasmed as she jerked her hips forcefully against mine. With each strong contraction of my orgasm, I sprayed four or five powerful squirts directly up the crack of her ass. My juices bounced off her buttocks and redirected over the front of my body, reaching as far as my face a couple of times. I wailed and thrashed my hips against Velvet as she held her long clit inside me for many long seconds. When we finally came down from our highs, she pulled her appendage out of me then she turned around and licked all the way up my vulva from my anus to my clit.

"That was good, baby," she said, winking at me with a sly smile. "Did you enjoy having your master's cock inside you?"

"Yes," I panted. "Thank you, master. I really needed that. Thank you for letting me come."

"It was my pleasure, believe me," she said, glancing up at the clock. "But we still have almost a full half hour left in your session. What shall we do with you with your remaining time?"

I looked at her with wide eyes, shaking my head. Whatever it was, I hoped it would involve more of this type of pleasure than the previous pain.

Velvet peered at my twitching pussy and paused. Then she steepled her fingers together and inserted her hand all the way into my hole up to her knuckles.

"As much as I enjoyed fucking you with my girl-cock," she said, "something tells me you're used to having *bigger* objects inside your tight cunny. Are you ready for a real man-sized cock now?"

I pinched my eyes at Velvet, unsure what she meant.

"No—I don't have a real man standing by to pleasure you," she laughed. "But I might have the next best thing."

She walked over to the far wall and lifted a blanket off a long piece of furniture nestled behind the throne chair. It was a square box with a long shaft extending horizontally out the end, with a giant dildo attached to the end. She grasped the metal shaft with one hand and tilted the box up on its end, then rolled it over in front of me.

"Have you ever tried one of these?" she said. "It's a fucking machine. My clients find it can be quite satisfying once they're properly warmed up. Do you think you can accommodate a slightly larger penis inside you?"

I looked at the giant dildo attached to the end of the rod and shook my head.

"That's a mighty big penis," I said. "How exactly does that thing work?"

"I'm sure you've experienced plenty bigger cocks than mine before," Velvet sneered. "It works just like a man does, providing forward thrust and pumping action. Let me show you."

Velvet pulled the device closer to my body, then strolled over to the handle in the middle of the floor. She pushed it away from her a few times, and my body ratcheted closer to the floor. When my pussy was about level with the height of the sex machine shaft, she returned to the box and flipped a switch on its upper surface. The metal bar began slowly pushing in and out of the box as the dildo thrust inches away from my dripping pussy.

My body instinctively turned away from the automated device as my eyes widened in fear. I wasn't quite ready to be fucked by a machine over which I had little control. Besides, the phallus attached to the end of the pushrod had to be at least ten inches long and three inches thick. I wasn't even sure it could fit inside me.

"What do you think, slave?" Velvet taunted. "Are you ready to be dominated by a new kind of master?"

"I'm not sure," I said, tentatively. "Exactly how deep and fast does this thing go?"

"That's entirely up to *me*," she said, lifting a remote-control device off the top lid and thumbing the control wheel forward.

As Velvet's smile grew progressively wider, the dildo began pumping faster and faster. Although my head was shaking no, my pussy was spilling a steady stream of love juices all over my ass.

"At least *one* part of you seems to like the idea," she said, noticing the cataract running between my legs. "Are you ready to give it a try?"

I nodded my head slowly, and Velvet pulled the device closer to me until the tip of the phallus was pressed against the entrance to my hole. Then she sat back on her chair and inched the flywheel forward with her thumb. I felt the dildo press harder against my opening, pressing my lips wider apart. Slowly, it inched further forward, spreading me wider apart. My eyes widened as I watched the huge cock slowly slide inside me until it was buried to the hilt. I moaned as it filled me up, surprised I could take its full length and girth.

"There now," Velvet said. "Doesn't it feel better to have a full-sized man cock inside you? Are you ready to be properly fucked now?"

"Yes," I nodded slowly.

I still wasn't sure I was ready to be fucked by such an imposing device while being tied up and in complete lack of control. But then I remembered I could utter my safe word at any time and stop the proceedings. Besides, Velvet would ultimately be in control of the device, and so far, she'd demonstrated reasonable restraint in subjecting me to unpleasant acts.

She pushed the control wheel forward, and the dildo began slowly pushing in and out of me. The silicone composition of the phallus made it soft and pliant, making it feel like a real man's penis. Before long, I began lubricating more freely and swaying my hips in tandem with the dildo's movement.

"I see you like being fucked by a *man*-cock too," Velvet smiled. "It looks like you swing both ways. Are you enjoying being filled up by a life-size penis?"

"Yes," I panted, feeling the big dildo spreading me open with each new thrust. "Fuck me with your man-cock, Mistress Velvet."

Velvet pressed the control wheel further forward, increasing the thrusting speed of the dildo. As I began writhing and moaning in my harness from the rising pleasure between my legs, Velvet placed her free hand around her erect clit and began jerking it up and down like a man.

"Fuck yes," I said, watching her get off watching me being fucked by her robot proxy. "Rub your big clit for me. I want to watch you cum again while I get fucked by this big cock."

Velvet slid down in her chair and spread her legs further apart as she thumbed the wheel forward another inch. The big dildo was now pistoning rapidly inside me, and I arched my back preparing to cum.

"Velvet," I panted. "Fuck me with your robot cock. I'm going to cum soon. Pound me harder."

Velvet pressed the flywheel forward as far as it could go as the dildo began cavitating rapidly inside me. With her mouth opened wide and her eyes glazed over, I knew she was on the precipice with me.

"Cum, baby," I said, temporarily forgetting the protocol of master and slave communications. "Let me see your pretty clit twitch and jerk with your orgasm."

Velvet removed her hand from her cocklet and she arched her back as she lifted her hips in the air. As I watched her ladycock flutter in spasms, I pressed my cunt forward as far as I could to press the big dildo against the back wall of my cavern. As it continued to pound in and out of me, I clamped down hard over the phallus and groaned out another long hard climax. Velvet watched me twist and jerk in my harness, her big chili pepper twitching and jerking as if applause of my accomplishment.

Suddenly, she reached down beside her chair and stood up holding a strap-on dildo. She quickly fastened it around her waist, then inserted her throbbing clit in the hollow end of the tube, then she turned off the fucking machine and yanked on the floor handle to ratchet me up to her height. Then, without warning, she thrust her big dildo inside me and began fucking me wildly. I was still coming down from last orgasm but the sight of her fucking me with the strap-on dildo quickly resurfaced the tingling between my legs and I soon felt another orgasm beginning to well up within me.

"Yes, Velvet," I screamed. "Fuck me harder. Make me come again, master. It feels good."

Velvet's eyes opened wide and she peered deeply into my eyes, looking at me like a wild animal. The hollow dildo was obviously providing some kind of direct friction for her also, and I could tell from her panting and hip action that she was on the verge with me.

"I'm going to cum again, master," I said. "Cum inside my hot cunt. Fuck me!"

Velvet grabbed the side of my harness and suddenly pulled me tight against her body as she pushed forward in one final powerful thrust.

"Uhnnn," she groaned, as I sprayed one last long stream of love juices all over her bare lips and asshole.

When we both finally stopping cumming, Velvet pulled

out of me and watched me swinging helplessly above the slippery floor. For the first time in almost two hours, I felt all the tension and stress of being bound and suspended in thin air slip away. I'd become fully satisfied being her submissive slave.

You can be anyone you want online...

NAKED YOGA

AN EROTIC ADVENTURE

VICTORIA RUSH

Mula Bandha is for lovers...

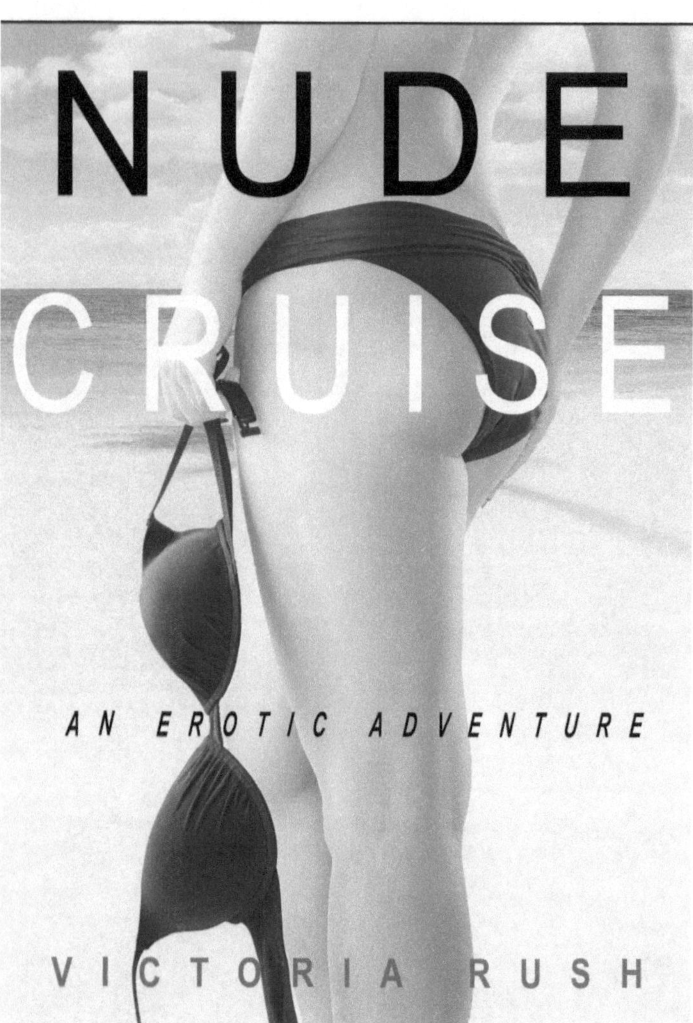

NUDE CRUISE

AN EROTIC ADVENTURE

VICTORIA RUSH

Some people get wet on a cruise for different reasons...

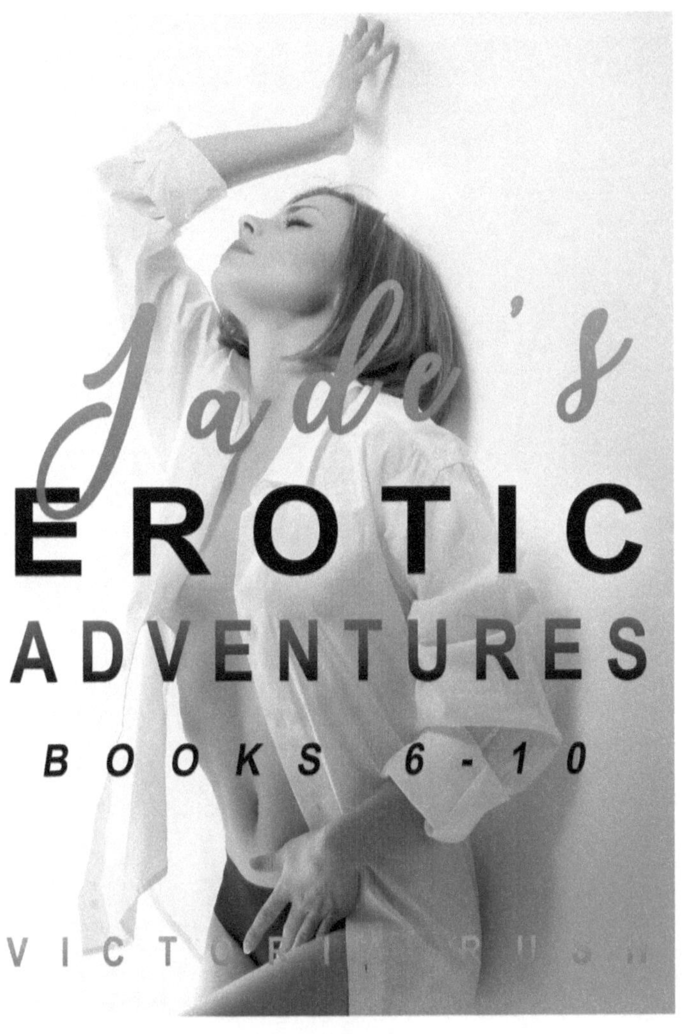

Books 6 - 10 in the bestselling series - now 60% off.

THE DINNER PARTY - PREVIEW

FINGER FOOD

Sometime later, I heard a soft tap on my bedroom door. Not wanting to remove myself just yet from my cocoon of luxury, I called out to answer.

"Yes?"

"It's time for your massage," a woman's voice replied.

"Just one minute please."

I reluctantly stepped out of the bath and quickly toweled myself dry. I wrapped a large bath sheet around me, re-donned my mask, then opened the bedroom door.

A petite young Asian girl greeted me, wearing a kimono similar to mine and a crimson masquerade mask.

Apparently not everybody who works here always walks around stark naked.

The girl was utterly breathtaking. Long jet-black hair cascaded over high cheekbones past pouty lips, her delicate collarbones peeking from the top of her kimono. I could see her breasts and hips outlined by the tightly-wrapped kimono and suddenly wished that she too had come to my boudoir naked.

"My name is Jasmine," she said. "I'm your personal

masseuse and esthetician. Are you ready for your final preparation?

Just the thought of this beauty laying her tender hands on me sent a shiver down my spine.

"Definitely. Please come in. How would you like me to prepare?"

"Come with me, please."

Jasmine led me into the bathroom, where she nonchalantly removed her kimono and hung it behind the bathroom door.

Oh my God.

I didn't think anyone in this place could get more beautiful or sensuous. Jasmine had perfectly shaped B-cup breasts with a thin indentation running down the center of her perfectly toned stomach. Like everyone else in this place, her pubis was utterly bald and flawless. She barely looked eighteen and I was just about to ask her age, but she spoke first.

"If you'd like to remove your towel and lay face down on the table, we can get started. May I call you Jade?"

There was something about her confident manner and tone that belied her youthful appearance. I had no inhibitions whatsoever about displaying myself unclothed to this stranger.

"Yes, thank you, Jasmine." I unhooked my bath sheet and threw it against the side of the tub.

"Would you like me to drape your backside?" Jasmine asked.

"That won't be necessary," I quickly answered.

Jasmine walked over to the vanity counter and picked up two small bottles of oil resting under an orange radiant lamp. She brought them back to the massage table, opened one, and poured the oil into one cupped hand then rubbed her hands together. The scent of lavender wafted toward my nose.

I closed my eyes in anticipation of her touch. I'd had massages before, but nothing as sensuous and stimulating as this. When her hands touched the small of my back, I jerked reflexively from the sexual tension. My heart was beating a hundred miles an hour as I felt the blood coursing through my veins.

Jasmine must have sensed my nervous tension and began pressing her fingers more firmly into my back as she moved them slowly up each side of my spine. The warm oil allowed her hands to glide effortlessly across my skin. She used every surface of her hands to massage my muscles, expertly kneading my skin with her fingers and palm.

I began to relax as my muscles softened and surrendered to her touch. She sensuously massaged every part of my back, shoulders, and neck, applying just the right amount of pressure. Periodically, she would pour more warm oil on my lower back, dipping her hands in it to replenish the silky lubrication against my pliant skin.

Just as the sexual tension began to subside from the utter relaxation of the massage, Jasmine moved her hands down to my buttocks and began to caress them in soft circular motions. My glutes contracted involuntarily and I unconsciously pressed my mound into the firm padding of the table. Suddenly I was quickly reminded that a gorgeous young woman was caressing my naked body. She cupped each buttock between her hands as she massaged my ass tantalizingly, her little finger sliding slowly into the cleft just above my anus.

Periodically, I'd partially open one of my eyes with my head turned in her direction to look at her gorgeous body. My head was at the same level as her midsection, and my mouth watered as I watched her stomach muscles flex and her hips undulate with each movement of her hands. At times her pussy was almost right beside me and I wanted to reach out and run my own fingers up her soft legs.

I was in total heaven and getting wetter by the moment. Just when I thought I couldn't stand it anymore, she suddenly moved her hands down to my feet and began massaging her thumbs into my soles.

I'd always loved having my feet massaged, but nobody did it like Jasmine. She cradled my foot and used every part of her hands to massage and knead every surface from my heel to my toes. I didn't want her to stop, but there were other parts of my body that were screaming for attention.

As if reading my thoughts, she began moving her hands up toward my calf, using her thumbs to spread the muscle apart. She lingered almost as long on my calf as she had on my foot, rolling the ball of my calf between both of her hands, sliding her slick hands up and down erotically. I couldn't help imagining how she might use those same hands to massage a man's erect cock in a similar manner. My mind wandered again to what pleasures lay in wait for me over dinner.

After shifting her hands to my right leg and giving my other foot and calf similar attention, she placed each hand just behind my knees and began to slowly move them up towards my buttocks. Her thumbs pressed against my inner thighs as she glided tantalizingly close to my apex.

I rolled my legs outward in an invitation to move closer. My legs were parted enough that I was sure she could see my vulva from her vantage point behind me. In my highly aroused state, my lips were engorged and spread apart, revealing my moist and quivering opening.

But as much as I desperately wanted her to, Jasmine

never touched me there. She repeatedly slid her hands right up to the edge of my slit, pressing and rotating her thumbs on the fleshy meat of my upper thighs just below my aching pussy. I suppose this was part of her master plan—to tease me mercilessly and inflame my passions so I'd be ready for just about anything at the main event.

It was certainly working. After thirty minutes of Jasmine's ministrations, I was grinding my pussy into the table trying desperately to give my clit some needed direct stimulation.

Just when I thought I couldn't be teased any more tantalizingly, Jasmine opened one of the bottles of warm oil and poured it directly into the crack of my ass. She paused as the fluid flowed down and directly over my parted lips. I almost came from the gentle movement of the warm liquid as it trickled across the folds of my labia, channeled toward the junction where they joined together at my clit. I shuddered in pleasure at the feeling, even if it was only the subtlest of touch.

Jasmine suddenly interrupted my thoughts.

"Would you like to turn over now?"

It was the first time she had spoken directly to me since the massage started, and it surprised me in my catatonic, pre-orgasmic state. I practically flipped over like a fish out of water and spread my legs expectantly. Finally, I'd get some relief. Surely, she couldn't leave me hanging like this.

"It's time for your final grooming," she said. "I'll need you to part your legs a bit further to provide full access."

Grooming? I knew this was part of the process, but somehow it didn't seem fair to transition at this precise moment. At least I'd be able to stay on the comfortable massage table instead of the clinical vinyl chairs used by my regular esthetician.

Jasmine walked over to another cabinet by the makeup table and withdrew a leather bag from one of the drawers, then brought it back to the table. She reached into the bag and pulled out a cordless hair trimmer.

"Do you have a preference regarding your appearance?" she asked. "Do you prefer natural, neatly trimmed, or bare?"

I knew she was referring to my pubic hair, which I generally kept neatly trimmed. I'd always thought going fully bald was unnatural and unseemly, catering to men's prurient fantasies of fucking young schoolgirls. But in this situation, it seemed entirely appropriate, like I was stripping away all my camouflage and armor.

If tonight was all about being watched, I might as well bare myself in every sense of the word and truly let my inhibitions go. I began to fantasize about rubbing my bare pussy against Jasmine's while she poured warm oil between us. The more work she had to do on me, the more chance I'd have to make this last and hopefully get off.

I didn't hesitate. "Bare, thank you."

"As you wish," she said. "I'll remove the long hairs first with the trimmer, then shave you smooth with a razor."

No waxing? This was different. I was relieved to not have to bear the painful and violent trial of having my hairs ripped out en masse. Although shaving down there was always a scary proposition, I felt safe in the capable and practiced hands of this beautiful esthetician.

Jasmine nodded, then flipped a switch on the trimmer. The device buzzed softly as she placed it gently on my mound. I had only a light dusting of fur and it didn't take long for her to remove it with a few short strokes over my pubis. I shuddered as the vibrations penetrated deep into my core. If she had placed the flat head on my clitoris, I would have popped off in a millisecond. Instead, she turned the trimmer face-down and gently swiped the vibrating teeth against the sides of my vulva, sensuously separating my labia with her hands as she moved the device between my legs to trim the hairs on the inside and outside of my labia.

It was an insanely titillating feeling, but just clinical enough to bring me down from my plateau and shift my focus. My mind wandered to the upcoming feast, and I contemplated what surprises lay in wait at the main event. The hostesses had suggested there would be 'contact' of some sort during the meal, and I was intrigued exactly who and how it would be administered. The idea of being fully bald, cleansed, and thoroughly stimulated going into the event was an incredible rush.

Jasmine continued with the trimmer all the way down my perineum to my anus, barely touching me with the trimmer so as not to pinch any delicate tissues. Apparently there were no parts of my erogenous zone that would remain untouched, now—and perhaps later.

She turned off the trimmer and placed it at the foot of the table. Then she took a bottle of gel from the bag and spread the gel on her hands. Using both hands, she spread it gently between my legs, starting on my mound all the way down to my rosebud.

My body almost levitated above the table as Jasmine finally laid her hands directly on my clitoris. The gel had a mild stinging quality that added to the stimulating sensation. If this was meant to excite my follicles in preparation for the shave, it wasn't the only feature of my anatomy that it made erect. I could feel the hood of my clitoris retract as my button filled with blood and began to push outward. Suddenly, I was fully stimulated again and lusting for Jasmine's touch. I fantasized about her bending down and taking my swollen nub between her puffy lips and letting me come in her mouth.

Unfortunately, my satisfaction would have to wait a little longer. Instead, Jasmine reached into her bag and pulled out a straight-edge razor. In anyone else's hands, it might look threatening, especially in my prostrated and vulnerable position. But something about the way she delicately and sensuously opened the jackknifed tool instantly evaporated my fears. I could see how this type of razor would in fact give her better control safely cutting my stubs instead of the usual ladies plastic razor.

With her right hand, Jasmine gently laid the razor on its flat edge at the top of my mound, while she gently pulled my skin upwards with her other hand. Then she slowly turned the sharp edge perpendicular to my skin and began softly scraping the razor downwards. I could hear the bristling sound as the razor edge removed my nubs right down to the follicles. She repeated the pattern in one inch wide swipes on one side then the other of my pubis, being ever-so-careful to stop just where my clitoris lay quivering in a mixture of fear and excitement. There was something about the utter vulnerability of the procedure that made it the most erotic experience I'd ever had.

Jasmine used the same deft touch as she moved down my vulva and perineum, scraping the vestiges of stray hairs away with gentle swipes of the long blade, while sensuously separating my folds and flesh with her other hand. She took extra time and care around my anus and clit, using the gentlest and slowest motion I've ever felt someone apply to my body. The combination of fright and titillation as she probed my most sensitive body parts created a river of sensuous fluids running down my vulva. By this time, no shaving gel was necessary to provide a smooth gliding surface for the knife.

When she was finished, Jasmine retrieved a fresh wash towel from beside the sink and held it under the warm water faucet then twisted the excess water into the basin. She returned to the table and placed it over my splayed legs then gently cleansed the excess moisture and remaining shaving gel with gentle massaging movements of her hands. The warm, moist towel felt exquisite against my newly shaved skin. Jasmine's hands now felt comforting between my legs rather than erotic.

She had taken me on an incredibly sensuous erotic arc, right to the edge of ecstasy and back, to a quiet relaxed place. I exhaled fully and completely for the first time in almost an hour.

Jasmine removed the towel from between my legs and held up a large hand mirror at a forty-five degree angle toward me.

"What do you think?" she asked.

I tilted my head up and studied her masterpiece. Far from the usual red and swollen vulva that I typically experienced after the violent waxing with my regular esthetician, I'd never seen my pussy look so beautiful. Utterly bereft of any hair, my entire perineum from my pubic mound to my anus was totally bald, pink—and gorgeous. I just stared at my beautiful pussy, utterly transfixed by the transformation.

"You have to *feel* it to really appreciate how beautiful you are, Jade," Jasmine purred.

I moved my right hand down, running my fingers along the edges of my pussy. I gasped from a feeling I'd never felt before. It felt smooth as silk: no bumps or blemishes or cuts or bruises. It was almost as if I was feeling somebody else— somebody I'd never felt before. I couldn't stop my left hand joining the other in rubbing and caressing my sensitive organs.

Jasmine lowered the mirror and smiled at me as I felt the moisture begin to accumulate between my legs again.

"It's almost time for your dinner appointment," she said. "Why don't you save the best for last? I think you'll find plenty of ways to satisfy your appetite over the next couple of hours."

She lifted my kimono from the hook at the edge of the bathtub and held it open for me.

"I'll escort you downstairs now if you're ready. All you need to bring is your kimono and slippers—and your mask of course."

I sat up slowly and stepped off the massage table. Turning around, I held my arms out as Jasmine lifted one arm of the silk robe onto me then the other. Then she turned around to face me, wrapped the silk tie around me, and tied a single bow over my belly button. She retrieved my matching silk slippers and knelt down on one knee to gently lift my feet one at a time and place them softly inside. It took every ounce of my power not to grab her head and pull it into my pulsating pussy.

Jasmine stood up gracefully and smiled into my eyes.

"If you'll follow me, I'll escort you now to the fantasy feast."

She didn't bother putting her own robe on. Her tight little ass barely jiggled as she stepped smartly ahead of me. I wasn't sure if I'd have a chance to feel Jasmine's touch again before the evening was over, but for now I was in total bliss ogling her petite, curvaceous figure from behind...

Read More

WEBCAM CHAT - PREVIEW

After my playdate with the dominatrix, I felt I needed a breather to regain control over my sex life. My little excursion into the world of BDSM had been fun, but being whipped and hog-tied by a domme had its limits. Now it was *my* turn to set the terms of engagement. I wanted to be back in the driver's seat and branch out beyond one dominant partner.

One lonely night at home, I sat down in front of my computer and began searching for some online fun. I wanted something different from the run-of-the-mill porn—something more engaging. I needed something involving a live, two-way interaction. With a real person, someone with whom I could share a genuine, passionate, if only temporary, relationship. A virtual *fuck buddy*, for want of a better word.

I typed in the search words *webcam sex chat* and a bunch of listings popped up for live online chat. I clicked on one labeled *LiveGirls*, and a gallery of videos showing scantily-clad women touching themselves filled the screen. I tapped one of the thumbnails, where a live stream showed a pretty girl lying facedown on a bed, wearing only a thong. As she swayed her hips from side to side, she looked over her shoulder suggestively toward the camera. Beside the video window, a flurry of comments filled the chat box.

Spread your legs, someone named bigjohn said.

Nice ass, hornyjoe commented.

Can I see your tits? guest34 pleaded.

All the while, the pretty brunette ran her hands across her concealed breasts and rolled her hips in the same robotic manner. For a moment, I was hypnotized like everyone else by her lithe and sexy body. But as attractive as she was, I had no interest in joining what amounted to a public strip show. I was just about to exit the screen when I noticed a button for Private Chat.

Let's see if she's any more engaging one-on-one, I thought.

I clicked the button and a Join Now window covered the stream.

Jeesuz, I cursed. They never make this easy.

I filled in the required fields for Username, Password, and E-mail, then clicked the button. The next screen presented me with a choice between selecting ten free credits or buying a package of credits starting at fifty dollars.

So that's how it works, I thought. *It's not much different from a real strip club. As long as you're stuffing their stockings with cash, the girls are happy to put on a show for you.*

I'd never paid for sex of any kind, and I wasn't about to get started now. I didn't want to chat with someone who was only in it for the money. I backtracked to the main search screen and adjusted my search phrase to *free amateur sex chat* and clicked Enter.

A fresh set of listings popped up, including an intriguing

one named *SexRoulette — free webcam live chat.* When I clicked on the link, a window came up with two side-by-side blank video screens. I enabled my laptop cam and mic, then I clicked the Start button. Suddenly, a live feed of me sitting half-naked in my bathrobe appeared in the left window, while some naked guy stroking his dick appeared in the right window.

Horrified to see that my face was showing, I quickly tilted my screen down and cursed out loud.

What's the matter? the naked guy typed in the chat box. *You're very pretty. Can I see your face again?*

I paused for a moment, realizing that he could hear me, then I clicked the microphone button to mute my mic. I wasn't prepared to carry on a live audio conversation with some naked guy. For that matter, I wasn't interested in carrying on a sex chat with *any* man.

I clicked the Next button and a different naked guy appeared with his legs spread wide apart, revealing another erect, throbbing cock. Every time I clicked Next, a different naked man appeared, pulling on his pud. As amusing as I found the experience of scrolling through a bunch of men's penises, the thought of chatting with one of these nameless guys turned my stomach.

Where were all the girls? I thought. *Are only guys interested in naughty online chats?*

I scanned the site and noticed some links across the top for different chat rooms. The default setting was for Mixed, but I could also choose between Guys, Girls, and Couples. Intrigued, I clicked on the Couples link, and a new window popped up showing a woman bobbing her head between a man's knees while his hand typed on a computer keyboard beside him on the bed.

Hi, the man typed in the chat window. *Wanna play?*

I paused for a moment, wondering if it might be fun to watch a hetero couple going at it.

Maybe some other time, I typed, before clicking on the Girls tab.

A new window popped up requiring me to verify that I was over eighteen years of age (*only to view girls??*) then I was redirected to a different website showing the familiar gallery of naked girls from the LiveGirls site. When I clicked on one of the images, a similar video and chat screen appeared. Another pretty young girl perched half-naked on a bed, while a bunch of anonymous viewers made lewd comments, 'tipping' her occasionally with tokens. Whenever anybody tipped her enough tokens, she bent over and waved her ass in front of the camera.

What the fuck? I thought. *Is it only professional girls who want to chat online?*

I clicked out of the website and was about to pull my vibrator out of my nightstand for some quiet alone time, when I decided to give it one last try.

There's got to be other lonely girls who are looking for a quick hookup with like-minded women.

I went back to the main search page and typed in *lesbian online chat.* Near the top of the listings, I noticed a site titled *SapphicChat — girls only free online chat.*

That's what I'm talking about, I said out loud, clicking the link.

Another side-by-side video setup appeared on the screen with a chat box underneath. I enabled my cam and carefully positioned my laptop lid so that only my torso was visible, then I pulled my robe tightly around my neck to cover myself up. There'd be no more skin showing until I was able to qualify a suitable candidate.

I clicked the Start button, and within a few seconds the

adjacent window flickered with a live stream showing a fat woman lying on her bed with her droopy boobs hanging down by her waist.

Yikes, I said, quickly clicking the Next button. I felt bad judging the visitors so harshly, but it wasn't much different from other dating apps. If you didn't feel the chemistry right away, everybody just moved on.

After a few seconds, a new image filled the sender window. This time an older woman sat in front of her computer with her elbows propped up on her desk. Deep folds of flesh hung from her neck and upper chest as she peered sadly into the screen.

Wow, I thought. *These online forums really bring out the lonely girls.*

I toggled through the list of online visitors until an image appeared showing a younger girl sitting cross-legged on her bed, wearing a tight V-neck sweater. Her breasts were full and plump, and although her face was partially hidden off-screen, I could tell from the downiness of her bare legs in a mid-thigh skirt that she was considerably younger than me. I parted my legs unconsciously as my pussy throbbed in excitement.

Finally. A sexy girl who wants an authentic online chat.

ASL? I typed, wanting to be sure she was of legal age. The last thing I needed was to have the police breaking down my door for engaging a minor in online sex.

19, curious, Houston, she typed. *You?*

Nineteen? She barely looked of age. I'd have to vet her more carefully if things went much further.

I paused for a moment, wondering how I wanted to present myself. I didn't want to scare her away by revealing my true age if she was looking to hook up with someone younger. But she had to lean at least a little bit toward girls if she'd engaged me this far.

28, bi, Milwaukee, I stretched the facts on all three aspects.

She paused for a moment holding her hand over her computer keyboard, then the video screen suddenly went blank and a new visitor came online.

Touché, I thought. *I guess this works both ways. My fellow online surfers can be just as rash and judgmental as me when it comes to who they find attractive.*

Obviously. I hadn't measured up in her eyes. But had I been too old, not the right sexual orientation, or was it my *body* she didn't like?

I peered at my image in my webcam feed and looked at my tightly-bound boobs wrapped up in my bathrobe. I'd been slouching a bit, and the heavy terrycloth robe wasn't doing much justice to the shape of my bosom. I spread the lapels of my robe a few inches apart and lifted my chest. My ample cleavage shone through the opening, revealing the roundness of my breasts.

That looks better, I smiled, nodding at the sexy reflection. *If this doesn't hook them, I'm really losing my mojo.*

The next visitor appeared to be another young girl seated on a chair in front of her computer. She only showed the lower half of her face, but from her tight skin and smooth neck muscles, she looked to be in her late teens or early twenties. Her tight T-shirt had a wishbone-shaped "C" emblem on the front. In the background, two small double beds sat on either side of her small room.

Hi, I typed, deciding to take a more measured approach with this new visitor. *What brings you to this crazy place so late at night?*

Just bored I guess, she responded.

Me too, I said. *This is my first time doing something like this. I'm used to meeting people the old-fashioned way.*

Boys or girls? she typed.

It was obvious that she was fishing. I had no idea what the right answer was, so I decided to play it safe.

Both, I guess. But I prefer girls. How about you?

I like boys... she typed. *But lately I've been finding myself unusually attracted to my dorm mate.*

Oh, I said, happy to hear she tilted both ways. *Where do you go to school?*

University of Chicago.

My heart skipped a beat when I realized how close she was to me in the real world.

What are you studying? I said, trying to steady my nervous hand as I typed.

I'm enrolled in the BA program, so right now it's mostly liberal arts. I'm just in my first year, so I haven't really decided on my major yet. I'm thinking maybe Communications...

She's barely eighteen! I thought. *My pussy throbbed at the thought of uncovering more of this pretty co-ed.*

What kind of career were you thinking of?

I dunno. Public relations, marketing, maybe television.

On the production side?

I suppose so. Somewhere behind the camera. I don't think I have prime time face.

You should let other people be the judge of that. From what I can see so far, I think you're very pretty. The combination of good looks and good communication skills will give you quite a leg up in that field.

Thanks, she said, tilting the camera up a little higher on her face. She smiled a broad smile, revealing perfectly-straight, pearly-white teeth. *What about you, what do you do?*

I'm a freelance graphic designer.

So you design websites and stuff like that?

A little bit of that. But I do more corporate work like logos, editorial layouts, that sort of thing.

That sounds interesting, the girl said. *I guess we both have an interest in communications of sorts...*

I paused for a moment, wondering how much longer I wanted to focus on the professional sides of our lives.

It looks like we share an interest in another form of communicating too. ;-)

LOL. This isn't the kind of communications my profs talk about.

I'm a little surprised to hear that, I said. *The world is rapidly adopting new forms of social media every day. Perhaps you can consider this as a type of vocational training.*

Except most people who come to this website are interested in only one thing.

You mean meeting people? I teased.

In a manner of speaking...

Are you testing the waters here because of your roommate?

Maybe. I didn't realize I had such a strong attraction to girls until I met her.

Have you shared your feelings with her?

Gawd no. She has a boyfriend. It could get very uncomfortable around here if I came on to her too strongly. We have to share this small room for the rest of the year and perhaps for the rest of our college residency.

Two charged up bodies in a small space can make for a combustible mixture. Do you think she's attracted to you also?

Not by the way I've seen her and her boyfriend go at it. I can't tell you how many times I've come back to my room to find a sock on the door.

Poor thing, I thought. *It doesn't sound like she's got much of an outlet to express her real feelings. I better tread lightly.*

Maybe you just need to be a little more suggestive when you have some alone time with her. You know, wear skimpier clothes to bed, come back from the shower naked. That sort of thing. If she's interested, she'll soon let you know.

It sounds like you have a little more experience with girls, she said. *Are you lesbian?*

Now we're getting to the crux of it, I thought. It was kind of fun playing the role of the girl's online mentor.

They say everyone's somewhere on the continuum, I said. *I'd say I'm about a nine, but I seem to be moving more to the right with each passing year. Men don't really do it for me any longer.*

The chat window paused for a moment as the girl seemed to process what I said.

What's it like? she said. *You know, being with a woman?*

Crikey, I thought. *How do I answer that without sounding like some kind of stalker?*

That's an interesting question. It's different in so many ways. Woman like different things than men. We're more focused on building the relationship. Men are mostly just inter-ested in sex.

Aren't women interested in that too?

Yes, of course, I laughed. *We just let it happen more —organically.*

Organically?

We let it happen naturally, as our feelings for one another grow stronger. Instead of just jumping on the biscuit, in a manner of speaking.

You mean kind of like what we're doing right now?

I was beginning to feel a strange attraction to this girl. Beyond the pretty outside package, she had a sweet inno-cence to her.

I suppose, I said. *We lesbians generally like to get to know our partner a little better before jumping into bed with them.*

Do you mind my asking how that works when you do get together? I mean, it's not like regular boy-girl coupling...

All this tip-toeing around the edges of sexy talk was beginning to stir some new feelings inside me. I was enjoying the process of educating this young girl on the nuances of lesbian relationships.

It's not so different, when it comes right down to it. We have the same sensitive parts. We just use them a little differently.

Do you miss the penetration aspect of the relationship?

Maybe it's time to stop being so nuanced, I thought.

Who says we have to forego the penetration aspect?

Oh, sorry—the girl said, as I saw a flush roll over her face. *It's just that without a penis involved in the equation...*

There are lots of ways us girls can enjoy penetration without a man. Strap-on dildos, two-sided phalluses, using sex toys. I'm guessing you've tried one or two of these before?

Well, yes. I have a vibrator I play with when my roommate is away. But I had no idea women used them together like you said.

Oh, yes. There are lots of interesting ways we make our own fun.

You're getting me pretty worked up talking about it. Can you tell me how you use a two-sided phallus?

Suddenly I became acutely aware of the wetness that had been accumulating between my legs. This innocent but sexy banter had been getting *both* of us worked up.

Well, usually it starts with us lying on our backs with our butts facing one another...

Mmm, the girl typed.

Fuck! I thought. *It's happening. I'm actually seducing a young college girl online!*

Then we insert the two ends in each of our pussies and push our bodies together...

The girl's left hand wandered below my line of vision as

she began to squirm in her seat while pecking her keyboard with her other hand.

All the way? she asked. *Do you touch your bodies together?*

Usually, if the dildo isn't too long. That's where it really gets fun. There's nothing so electrifying as feeling your lover's peachka pressed up against your own.

God, that's so hot!

And wet. ;-)

You're making me very wet right now.

I spread my legs and began strumming my clit with my fingers at the thought of the pretty co-ed getting turned on by my explanation.

Are you touching yourself? I said.

Yes. Are you?

I am now.

I wish I could touch you the way you're describing right now.

If I could reach out through my screen, believe me, I would. I'd love to show you what it feels like to make love to a woman.

Can I see your breasts? They look very full and sexy.

I thought you'd never ask.

I pulled my robe apart and let the shawl fall around my shoulders.

OMG! the girl typed. *They're gorgeous. Do you mind if I ask how old you are? Because those are the most beautiful tits I think I've ever seen.*

I paused for a moment trying to decide how young I wanted to pretend to be. The last thing I wanted to do in the heat of the action was scare away another online partner because she thought I was too old.

Everybody tells me I look ten years younger than my real age, I thought. *She'll never know.*

That's very kind of you, I said. *I'm twenty-five. But before we go any further, I should probably ask you the same. If you're in your first year of college, you must be barely legal.*

I turned eighteen two months ago.

Like I said. Barely legal.

We're two consenting adults.

Since we're getting to know each other so intimately, can I ask your name? I don't want to have sex with a faceless, nameless person.

I'm Holly.

Pleased to meet you Holly. My name's Jade.

That's a lovely name.

Yours too, I said. *Holly and Jade. I like the way they go together.*

I'm imagining us going together in more ways than one.

Damn, girl, you're making me soaking wet. Can I see a bit more of you too? I want to let my mind run all over your sweet body.

The girl reached up over her shoulders and pulled her T-shirt over her head. Then she reached behind her back and unclasped her bra. When she pulled it off her shoulders and threw it on the floor, I gasped. Her breasts were smaller than mine, but stood firm and erect on her chest. But far more fascinating, was their *shape*. They were far pointier than most, pressing straight out toward me like two fleshy obelisks.

Mmm, I typed. *Those are mighty succulent boobies you have, Holly.*

Not as full and appetizing as yours! she returned.

I love their shape. I could suck on your pointy nipples all day!

I'd like that, Holly said. *You're going to make me cum pretty soon if you keep talking to me like that.*

That's not the only part of you that I want to suck, I said, starting to rub my clit more quickly. *I want to take your sweet nub into my mouth and watch your twist all over my face.*

Yes, Jade. I want you to suck my clit. Make me cum all over your face.

Oh Baby, I said. *Let me see and feel you cum. I'm pressing my fingers inside you now...*

Fuck, Jade. I can feel you inside me. I'm going to cum...

As I watched Holly writhing in her chair, my mouth opened unconsciously, imagining her riding my face.

Yes, baby, I said. *Cum in my mouth. Let it go.*

Suddenly, a deep flush spread over Holly's chest and she began jerking wildly in her chair.

Ohhhhhhh, she typed. *I'm cumming Jade!*

I hadn't been concentrating very much on my own feelings up to this point, but when I saw Holly coming, I thrust my fingers deep into my pussy and gushed all over my hand. While I watched her jerking in her chair, my tits jiggled spastically on my chest as the tremors spread throughout my body.

After a long pause, Holly began to type again.

That was incredible! she said. *I haven't had an orgasm that powerful in a long time.*

You should try this girl thing more often, I typed. *It's even better in real life. Maybe you and your roommate can find a way—*

Suddenly, Holly's face turned to the side and a panicked expression fell over her face.

I think she's here! she typed. *Someone's at the door!*

Oh no—not now, I thought. *Just when we were establishing such a strong connection.* I banged away at my keyboard, fearful of losing her forever.

Can we do this again some—

Holly's video stream suddenly went dark as she signed

out of the program. I was sad to see her go, but at the same time I was thrilled to have made such an exhilarating connection my first time online.

I'm going to have to try this again very soon, I thought, closing my laptop with sticky fingers.

Read More

ABOUT THE AUTHOR

If you would like to receive notification of new books in Jade's Erotic Adventures, follow me at http://bookbub.com/authors/victoria-rush.

If you have a moment, please post a brief review on my Amazon book page at mybook.to/td . Even just a couple of sentences will help other readers find and enjoy this book as much as you hopefully did.

Follow, share, like, and comment at:

www.facebook.com/authorvictoriarush
www.pinterest.com/authorvictoriarush
www.twitter.com/authorvictoriarush
authorvictoriarush@outlook.com

Hope to see you again soon!

www.ingramcontent.com/pod-product-compliance
Lightning Source LLC
Chambersburg PA
CBHW030821200726
48288CB00004B/1329